I AM LEAPER

I AM LEAPER

by **Annabel Johnson**

illustrated by Stella Ormai

AN
APPLE
PAPERBACK

SCHOLASTIC INC.

New York Toronto London Auckland Sydney

ISBN 0-590-43399-7

Text copyright © 1990 by Annabel Johnson.
Illustrations copyright © 1990 by Scholastic Inc.
All rights reserved. Published by Scholastic Inc.

APPLE PAPERBACKS is a registered trademark of Scholastic Inc.

12 11 10 9 8 7 6   3 4 5 6/9

Printed in the U.S.A.   40

For Haydn
(who loves the desert, too)

1

It was a very nice cage. There was a food dish and a water dish and a layer of wood chips on the floor. There was even an exercise wheel where you could run in circles all day, if you like that sort of thing. They had left her a supper of seeds, but she hadn't eaten any. She was curled up in the corner — a small clump of light brown fur not much bigger than a golf ball, neatly wrapped in a long tail that ended in a tuft, like a lion's. From behind this, she watched.

And so she was aware the minute they opened the door of the cage. She could have made a break for freedom. The cage was on a lab table — that would have been no problem to her. The door of the lab was closed, but there was a crack under it. She was good at cracks. And her speed was faster than the swoop of an owl. It had to be.

She didn't run because she hadn't come here to escape. She needed help. She hoped she could talk to them, these two huge men in their white coats. Ever since they had brought her to this place of prisoners, she had tried to get their attention. They didn't seem to understand.

Now they were bringing in a new creature, square and gray and hard-looking. She wouldn't have thought it was alive, but when she ventured out of the cage and over to it, she could feel it pulsing. From one side came a long, snake-like wire with a round tube on the end. She realized that it

2

must be an ear because one of the men spoke into it.

"Study of animal communication, test number six, rodent series: *Dipodomys merriami*, also called 'kangaroo rat.'"

Strange words — she didn't recognize her scientific name. She only knew the man had laid the ear down on the table close to her, like an invitation. She spoke into it, a cautious squeak, and the creature's square green face lit up.

One of the men peered at it. "Test impossible to render phonetically." He read the words and frowned. Then he began to poke at the square scales on the creature's chest, muttering to himself. "Reduce pitch . . . reset to ultra slow. . . ."

The other man looked troubled. "We didn't run into this kind of problem with the gopher and the mouse."

That amused her. Mice can only speak their own language, which is fairly simple.

Gophers are limited, too; they can barely talk to other gophers. Very few animals have the gift of tongues. That's why she had been chosen. By all the denizens of the desert, she had been picked to warn these people. Somehow, she just had to make them understand.

The gray creature seemed willing to listen. Again she twittered into the round ear as carefully as she could. She felt the thing puzzling. It lowered the pitch (for her voice was higher than the human ear could comprehend). It slowed the sounds (for she talked a hundred times faster than people do). At last, a single bright line appeared across its face.

The two men stared at it, their eyes wide with shock. Slowly, one of them read the words aloud as if he couldn't believe it:

"I am Leaper."

2

The laboratory was so quiet you could hear the drip, drip of the tap, over in the sink. All around the big room the caged animals were listening, watching, because each of them had tried to speak to these men, and failed.

The gopher had pleaded in his own tongue, *Let me go, let me go. . . .*

The chipmunk had scolded, *How dare you lock me up?*

And the mouse had simply cried, *I'm scared!*

The blackbird had used some very bad words, and the sad bat in the corner cage just hung there upside down, pretending to ignore everybody.

The human beings hadn't understood any of these messages. Neither had the machine — it was only programmed to listen in English. And that is exactly what Leaper had spoken.

The two men stood staring at the screen. "The computer must be malfunctioning." The one who said that was a thin man, pale as a peeled parsnip. You could hardly tell where he left off and where his white lab coat began. His name was Whitman.

"Or a coincidence? It's probably a coincidence. Similar phonetics that the computer turned into words by chance." The other man was named Harrison, though everyone called him "Harry," probably because he was — very hairy, from the curly top of his head right down through his eyebrows to his beard. It was thick and brown, and in it his mouth looked like a red raspberry in a bowl of shredded wheat.

"I'll cross-check with the other data," he said and began to punch some more keys. The machine hummed as it reached into its memory bank to find the gopher's test:

"EEEEE-Yuk-Yuk!"

"Now try the mouse," Whitman suggested, and the computer produced the mouse's test:

"CHEEEEEE-Yike!"

"Everything seems to be functioning properly," he said. "All we can do is repeat the experiment."

Leaper sighed to herself and spoke once more into the creature's ear. After a few seconds it translated her chitter into words:

"I am Leaper. I have come to
talk to you about a matter of life
and death."

7

Harrison's little red mouth began to grin. "This is incredible. In-credible! A kangaroo rat that speaks English. We've made a complete breakthrough." And he went to the coffee maker and poured himself a big steaming cup.

More cautiously, Whitman said, "What we have is a rodent that *appears* to be making sounds that *seem* to imitate human speech, and if you don't stop drinking that stuff, you will give yourself the jitters."

But Harrison already had them. He was striding around the room. (He didn't realize how large and loud his feet sounded to the prisoners down in the lower cages — the tarantulas were terrified.) "We'll be the talk of the scientific world," he said. "Even the unscientific world. This is national news. We ought to call a press conference."

In a parsnippy voice, Whitman told him, "That would be a very bad idea right now. Consider what publicity would mean — the place would be crawling with journalists and photographers and other strange people. We haven't even got a security system."

Harrison stopped in his tracks. "You're right! This specimen is a valuable piece of property. We'd better get it back in its cage." He reached out to seize Leaper in his big blunt hand.

And suddenly — she wasn't there. She had shot sideways in a leap of twenty-seven inches. (Not one of her greatest, but then Harry was no owl.) The instant she hit the floor she ducked into the nearest hiding place, a tangle of soft thick stuff that was attached to a pole.

This mop was held by a boy who had been standing so still in the corner the men had forgotten him. His name was Julian X. Jones. The "X" stood for Xerxes, which wasn't his fault. His mother had picked the name out of a book because it meant "king" and she thought it might bring him luck. But she called him "Red" for the carrot-colored hair that flopped around his ears. His father called him "J. X.," which made him feel cool, and rather grown-up.

It was his dad who had got him this after-school job at the Environmental Research Center. Julian's father worked here, too, as a photographer. Right now, he was away on a field trip taking pictures of the desert fauna and flora (another name for animals and plants, but scientists prefer things to sound complicated). This was the boy's first job. He knew he was too young for it, so he spent a lot of time staying out of the way. He kept quiet, too; at 12¾ years old, you aren't supposed to have opinions — the two researchers had made that clear several times. But right then he was the only one in the room who knew where Leaper had gone.

Whitman got downright irked at Harrison. "You should not have let it loose on the table."

"But they test better that way." Harry was

searching behind the jars and books and reptile boxes. (He made such a bustle, the garter snakes coiled up like a bunch of shoe-laces.) "Never mind, we'll find it, we'll find it."

Whitman never was one to rush around. He stood in the center of the room with his arms folded and just looked, and looked . . . until all at once he said, "Ha!" It was her tail that gave Leaper away. Two inches of

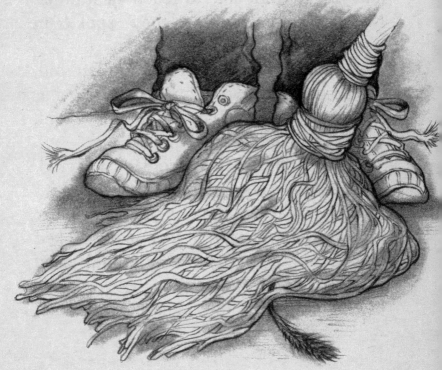

it stuck out in plain view. "It's under the mop. Don't move a muscle, boy, stand still. I've got a net in the closet."

Julian couldn't help thinking that nets are rather nasty. He bent over to offer Leaper his hand instead. His palm looked steady. Politely she hopped onto it. And at that, a strange thing happened: As if their minds were connected by a telephone line, Leaper and Julian were able to reach each other. No need for words — they spoke in thoughts.

From the depths of his head, Julian said, "Hello, friend, I won't hurt you."

And Leaper's small brain replied, "Thank you. Please don't squeeze."

Meanwhile the two scientists hovered, hesitating to grab her for fear she might leap out of reach again. She was balanced on her long hind legs, her front feet neatly tucked up under her fur as usual, her tail quivering like a live wire.

"Put her . . . in the . . . cage," Whitman

said very slowly, as if he were addressing a little child. "Just . . . take it . . . easy. . . ."

Julian thought it would only be proper to get Leaper's opinion. His mind asked her, "Where do you want to go?"

"I'd like to speak to the one-eared creature again," she replied. "I must make these people listen."

Julian's lips twitched in a smile, part doubt and part sympathy. "Lots of luck," he wished her silently, as he set her back on the table.

3

Now Whitman really was in a snit! His words exploded like a pan of popcorn. "I knew we never should have taken on a helper this young. Boy, didn't you hear me? I said to put the specimen in the cage. This is your first job, so I won't fire you yet, but you've got to learn to obey orders."

And Harrison scowled with both hairy eyebrows. "If you ever want to amount to anything, you'd better learn to *listen*. You've got the ears for it."

Julian X. Jones could feel his ears turning red. They really were rather large; he could always feel people noticing them. But he forgot his embarrassment as Leaper hopped over to the microphone and began to chatter into it.

The computer mused and modified, then repeated her words:

"I, Leaper, having the gift of
tongues, have been sent here by
the denizens of the desert to ask
your help with a terrible problem."

The men stared at each other, speechless. At last, Harry said, "We must discover how it learned this trick. I mean, who taught it to parrot these words? Was it someone's pet?"

Desperately, Leaper gave a bunch of small screeches:

"I learned by listening.
I listen to the people-who-picnic.

15

I listen to the people-who-collect-
rocks.
I listen to the teachers-who-bring-
children on field trips to the
desert."

And over in his corner, Julian hoped Harrison would be impressed by all that listening.

But the scientists were too excited to pay
attention to what she said. "By george,"
Whitman marveled, "this may get us a gov-
ernment citation. To say nothing of an in-
creased budget."

And Harrison added, "We might even get
funds to hire an assistant — someone who
can make halfway decent coffee." He was
getting the jitters again.

Meanwhile, Whitman had gone over to
unlock the closet. "It is important to estab-
lish that the specimen is legally ours," he
said. "It must have once belonged to someone else around here, who taught it this

trick of speaking. There's no way I know of that you can copyright a rodent, but we can document ourselves by getting it all down on tape, for the record."

"Darned right," said Harrison. "Finders, keepers." He began to set up the video camera. "Can you imagine what Disney Studios would pay for the rights to film a talking kangaroo rat?"

Leaper tried to get their attention with a question:

"What's a kangaroo?"

Nobody took her seriously except Julian, who explained in a low tone, "It's a large animal that hops long distances on its back feet." And that, of course, was exactly why she was known by this odd name, because she, too, used only her hind legs to make those mighty leaps. He was admiring them when Harry snapped him out of it.

"Don't just stand there, boy, help me set up these lights."

Fierce spotlights, they hurt Leaper's eyes. The brightness and the noise and the crowded room were making her sick with disappointment. Turning away sadly, she hopped back into the cage and burrowed down into the wood chips. She curled into a tight knot, vowing never to speak a word to them again. She had offered herself up in their trap, she'd been taken from her native land, she had lost her home forever — and all for nothing.

No one was even slightly interested in hearing about the Monster.

4

All afternoon the men tried to make her
talk. She wouldn't even mumble a chirp
from behind her tail. They finally gave up
and went home. Then, as darkness fell, Julian Jones came out of his corner to mop
the floor in long, slow sweeps so as not to
disturb all the small wild things in their
cages. They weren't asleep — most of them
liked the nighttime best, when the lab was
dim and deserted. They stirred around and
even got a bit hungry. To each one he
brought fresh food and water. When he

came to Leaper, he saw she hadn't touched her seeds.

"Little friend," he said, "if you don't eat, you will die."

She made a small noise like a dry leaf cracking.

"I can't understand unless you come and touch." He held out his hand.

She hopped into it. She didn't really want

to talk, but this boy had been kind to her. When their minds connected, she felt his concern. "It's no use," she told him. "These seeds taste awful. I can't stand them."

"Then I'll get you some other kind," he promised. "Something you'll like."

"For that, you'd have to go to my home. It is a long way from here. I'm not even sure I could find my way back. They put me in a box" — she shuddered at the memory — "I couldn't see a thing."

"Never mind. Tell me what signs to look for and I'll find the way."

Leaper thought hard. Not that she didn't remember it well. She could see every pebble and blade of grass, and the way the sun filtered through the ancient tree by day and the shadow of the owl on a moonlit night. But how to tell it? At last she formed the words mentally:

"Go until you come to a vast land where there are no walls, but many windows. It is silent, but the stillness seems loud.

"Through this country a number of rivers run, but not with water. Follow the largest until it grows small.

"You will come to a chimney without a house. On one side of it there's a cave with a black heart, but its veins run blue. Beside the mouth of the cave, the life-bush grows, though it will appear to be dead. The sand beneath will be full of life-seeds.

"And finally" — she felt she'd better warn him — "you must watch out for the Monster."

"Monster?" Julian thought he knew what she meant. "A Gila monster? Don't worry, I've seen plenty of those. In fact, there's one in a box right over here." He took her to view the sullen reptile, chomping its ration of hard-boiled eggs.

"Old Stink-breath?" She was scornful. "That's just another ugly lizard. The crea- ture I refer to is a thousand times bigger and meaner. *His* breath can kill you! He comes from the Black River and they say that's deadly, too. Don't go near it. And if you hear an awful cry out across the desert, hide. You're too young to face the beast all by yourself."

The lab seemed chilly with shadows, but Julian swallowed his taste of uneasiness. Leaper needed those seeds. Crouched in his hand she was as light as matchsticks. She couldn't afford to go without many more meals.

"Don't worry," he told her briskly, "I'll take a spin out to the desert tomorrow. It's my day off. I'll bring back the seeds. And if this Monster shows up, I'll — just — handle him, that's all."

5

By the next morning Julian felt up to a good adventure. The little town where he lived was just a sprawl beside the big interstate highway, mostly motels and gas stations — not all that exciting. The biggest building in town was the Environmental Research Center. The men didn't work there on Saturdays, so he could take the day off. And he usually spent it riding his dirt bike.

Just a small one, it wasn't much good for moto-cross, but he practiced his techniques on the sandy humps out behind his house.

And sometimes he went on a cross-country run. So his mother didn't think it was unusual when he filled his thermos with water and put a peanut-butter sandwich in his backpack. His folks had long since taught him to be careful, and they trusted him.

It was easy to parallel the highway — the one that the scientists always took when they went out trapping. (They called it "collecting specimens," but to Julian, a trap was a trap.) In the bright hot sunlight he bounced along across the vast vacant country; it reached away on all sides clear to the horizon, which was rimmed by rocky hills.

There wasn't much greenery — a few stunted paloverde trees, all twigs and no leaves. Down in the dry washes, an occasional ironwood tree was more gray than green. Of course there were plenty of creosote bushes — they could live in the worst soil because their roots reached fifty feet down to find water. And cactus, he saw plenty of prickly pear.

But mostly the desert was just rock and sand, flat except where the broad arroyos cut through it. One of them had banks so steep, Julian decided to walk his machine over to the highway and cross on the low bridge there. He couldn't ride the motor-bike on the highway because he wasn't old enough to get a license. Too young again. Too young for practically everything. Julian brooded, but not for long.

As he reached the bridge he noticed a signboard that had faded until the letters couldn't be read. But it must mean that this was a major arroyo. The bottom was dry, just a torrent of sand that flowed around islands of rock and drifted against the banks — a river without water. That must be what Leaper meant!

He started to ride along the bank, but it occurred to him — if this Monster was around, it might be wiser to go quietly. He parked in a narrow crevice and looked for some brush to cover the machine. Then, as he was about to pull some up, he recalled what Leaper had said about things that looked dead but were not.

Until I know what a life-bush looks like, he thought, I'd better leave all of these alone.

Already working up an appetite, he polished off the sandwich. Then he took his thermos of water and clipped his flashlight to his belt. He had brought the Big Beam because he had a hunch he just might find himself a cave.

As Julian set off along the bottom of the draw, for a while he could hear the swish of cars back on the highway. But in a few minutes he had left all people-sounds behind. Then the silence crept in. It pressed up on him from all sides — such miles of it, such tons of it, his ears began to ring. It was as if all the quiet in the world was stacked in this one place. It almost seemed to dare him to make some noise if he could.

"YAAAAA-A-A-HOOOO!" He gave a wild cowboy yell. But in that ocean of stillness, it didn't make a splash.

He had never walked through a place so empty. Under the hot sun not a creature stirred, not a bird or an insect, unless you count a few ants. Back closer to town, there was always the arguing of sparrows, the lazy loop of a butterfly. This far out, it was as if he had stepped onto a stark, unfinished planet, or maybe a very ancient one that had begun to crumble.

The shelving shoulders of the wash were riddled with holes. There were burrows leading down under the rocks — he imagined Leaper had lived in one. But most of them looked dark and deserted. Even the barrel cactus had a hole in it. Julian bent over to look closer. . . . And inches away from his eye, another eye blinked at him blackly. He jumped back so fast he got sand in his shoes. When he took a more cautious

look, he could make out a long, sharp beak. Sitting quietly in there, a small bird was ready to peck his nose.

All at once, a whole new prickly sensation came over him — of being watched from all sides. Not alone at all! He was in the middle of a whole different world. When he walked closer to the face of the rocky bank, he heard a swift scramble of small feet far back inside. A thousand tunnels and passageways made this a desert apartment house, and these holes were its windows, which Leaper had mentioned. Behind them lived a mysterious populace. He could feel it breathing.

6

Uneasy as a trespasser now, Julian walked slowly on. The blaze of noon was making the arroyo shimmer with heat ripples. Up ahead, the gulch split into four branches — no way to tell which was the main one. Wiping the sweat from his eyes, he drank some water from the thermos and began to search the ground for a clue.

In the third of the gullies, half hidden in the sand, he picked up a chunk of stone darker than the others, almost black. Across it ran a narrow thread of blue, like a vein.

He glanced around but couldn't see a cave. Still, it was the only lead he had so he put the stone in his pocket and followed that arm of the arroyo.

As he approached a bend, he heard voices. And the next moment, out of the sand near his feet, there burst a furry animal — it looked like a squirrel with an unsuccessful tail. At the sight of him, it gave a squeak of shock and raced away down the wash.

Rounding the bend, Julian saw what it was escaping from: A large shaggy brown dog had been digging up its burrow. Beyond was a family of rock hunters. At least he guessed that's what they were, a mother and father and two young girls searching the ground, stowing pebbles in their knapsacks. When the dog saw Julian it rushed at him, barking ferociously, making horrible faces. A big bully of a hound — could that be Leaper's Monster? There was no time to wonder. He had to concentrate on looking like a statue. He was glad he had practiced standing still until he had it down to an art. It puzzled the dog, who preferred to see people run away in terror. It's hard to have much fun with someone who doesn't move.

"Come here, Zorro!" the father of the family called. The mother got out a leash while the children began to show off, the way little kids do.

One girl was yelling, "We're on a rock hunt!"

And the other cried, "I found a piece of turquoise!"

"Be quiet about that," her father snapped. "You want everybody on earth trying to beat us to it?"

"Not me," Julian said. "I don't know one stone from another. Is it valuable?" He was fingering the piece in his pocket.

"Oh, turquoise can bring big money if it's good quality." The father couldn't resist explaining to a person who didn't know a thing. "These small chunks aren't worth much, but they had to wash down from a larger deposit above here. If I can find that, I'm going to stake a claim and mine the stuff."

"Go for it," Julian said, his face very straight, because he had noticed — well, never mind. He could keep his mouth shut.

As soon as they had gone off up the gulch, he walked across to the narrow cranny he had seen. It ended in a pocket of rocks, like a three-sided chimney. And almost out of sight, far at the back, was an opening — like the mouth of a tunnel. Pitch-dark inside, it was as black as Leaper had described it.

He unhooked the flashlight, shining the beam ahead of him as he crawled through the low entrance . . . and found himself surrounded by the most delicate blue network of turquoise that ever laced the walls of a hidden cave.

7

After the blistering sun, the cave felt wonderfully cool. Julian Jones sat down on a large stone and looked around. The cave wasn't very big, only about ten feet across, but the veins might go deep into the rock — who knows how far? For five minutes he went on a spree. In his daydream, he filed claims and mined and sold turquoise and bought himself a sports car and became a Man of Importance. But he couldn't really see himself in a blazer and a silk scarf.

So then he became a Man of Science and

set up his own laboratory. He hired Harrison and Whitman to be his assistants — he made them mop the floor. But that was only fun temporarily. The truth was he didn't much like rooms full of cages. It dawned on him: *He hated cages!*

What he'd rather do, he thought, was live right here in the turquoise cavern, instead of tearing it down and selling pieces of it. This was a good cave. Very safe, rent-free, and it certainly was nicely decorated. With his own window looking from the inside out, he began to feel part of that secret world. *Me, a denizen.*

He tried the idea on, but it didn't quite fit. He knew if there was a choice between a diet of seeds and a slice of pizza, he'd pick the pepperoni. But there were times in his life when he wouldn't mind hiding out for a few hours in a secret place. He finally decided, *I am never going to tell a living soul about this cave.*

And from somewhere, an alien mind

broke through to touch his. "Young fool . . . hrrrump . . . may have some intelligence after all . . . grrrump!"

It wasn't like his easy contact with Leaper. This transmission came muffled, as if through several inches of bone. Julian glanced around, flashing the light into the corners. "Who are you? Have we met?"

"In a way . . . hrrrump . . . I've become acquainted with . . . your rrrump. . . ."

Julian jumped up so fast he bumped his head on the top of the cave. Turning the light, he saw that he'd been sitting on not a rock, but a large, elderly tortoise. "Excuse m-m-me," he stammered. It was embarrassing to have sat on a stranger. "I'm very sorry to intrude in your cave. I dropped by to pick up some seeds for Leaper."

The tortoise blinked its moody eyes. But its thoughts didn't come through until Julian laid a respectful hand on its scaly head. "Could you repeat that, please?" he asked.

"Got herself trapped . . . chummmp . . .

as if anyone could stop the Monster . . . ugggghh . . . beast killed my cousin. He always was a bit slow . . . mmmmph."

Julian couldn't imagine how a dog had managed to murder a turtle, but he felt the old creature didn't want to talk about it. "If you could direct me to Leaper's life-bush I'd be obliged."

"You broke a twig off when you . . . glummmmphed . . . in here." The tortoise pulled its head and legs up under its shell, and was silent. The conversation was over.

Being extra careful this time, Julian crawled back out. He hadn't even noticed the bush before. It looked dead, all right. Scraping up the sand beneath, he sifted it through the scrap of fine screen he'd brought along for the purpose. Again and again he sifted, while the sun sank low, leaving purple shadows along the bottom of the gulch.

A sudden rush of wings almost brushed his ear. Julian started up to see a shadow

39

skim the rim of the arroyo. An owl, he thought, but it was already too dark to be sure. He had never known evening to come on so fast. The whole sky had dimmed like smoked glass, darkening to deep violet except for one last fiery streak far to the west.

The mysterious depths of the earth were beginning to stir, as if the denizens were preparing to come forth. Feeling more than ever like an intruder, he turned and headed back down the wash in a hurry. All at once, he missed people. He missed traffic and cassette players and McDonald's — he was awfully hungry. And tired. And there was sand in his shoes.

But in his pocket, in a matchbox, he was bringing Leaper seventeen seeds.

As it turned out, those seeds cost Julian four blisters, twenty-nine aching muscles, and almost his job. He took inventory while lying in bed that next morning. He knew his legs would unstiffen, and he could put Band-Aids on the blisters. The worst problem was an emptiness of pocket. He was down to his last two dollars and thirty-seven cents, barely enough to buy gas for the bike. So he really needed that job. And for a minute, he had thought he'd lost it.

They had caught him feeding Leaper. At

7:45 in the evening he had slipped into the lab past the night watchman, who was doing crossword puzzles and didn't consider him a threat to security anyway. He'd gone to the specimen room and let Leaper out of her cage, and all of a sudden he had found himself surrounded.

Harrison had come slip-slopping in, wearing his bedroom slippers. Whitman wore a lab coat over his bathing suit — he'd been taking a dip in the swimming pool of the building where the research personnel lived, just across the street from the Center. His long pale shanks ended in beach shoes and would have looked funny if his face hadn't been so grim.

"I saw the lights on in here," Harrison was ranting and raving. "I knew something was wrong."

And Whitman demanded, "Exactly what do you think you're doing with that rat, young man?"

"I just brought her some of her own kind

of seeds," Julian tried to explain.

"Oh, so now we have a naturalist on our staff. And when did you get to be an expert on animal nutrition? I told you never to feed these specimens unauthorized food. Let me see those!"

But Leaper had crammed the rest of the life-seeds into her cheek pouch and dived back into the cage.

That made Whitman even angrier. "You don't seem to be able to follow orders, boy. Can you think of one good reason why I shouldn't fire you?"

Julian thought fast. "Because you need me to mop the floor tomorrow?"

The two scientists gave him very dark looks and went into the office to discuss it. They must have decided he had a point, because when they came back they said he could stay.

"But you'd better not make one more mistake!" Harrison waved his hand, and the blackbird, thinking a hawk was after him, nearly had a nervous fit. "Don't you *dare* touch that rat again. We'll be keeping an eye on you."

And they could do it. The apartment building faced the Research Center. They could see everything that went on, including what time he came to work.

On Sundays it was Julian's job to mop the lab, see that the water dishes were full, and put fresh wood chips on the floors of the cages. That particular morning, as he hauled his sore shanks out of bed, he thought he'd better shape up. "I'm not going to experiment around any more," he decided. "It's the truth — I am not a naturalist. I'm no expert on animals, or anything else."

By the time he got to work he was so low in spirits you could have pulled his socks up over his ears. He took the water pitcher, filled it, and started around the cages full of specimens. He was going to think of them as specimens from now on, so he wouldn't get involved in their personal problems.

But when he came to Leaper, she sat there looking up at him, going "Chit, chit, chit . . ." What could he do? He held out his hand. The minute she touched it, he sensed that she was happier. "So good, so good, the seeds were so good! I never thought I'd taste them again. How did you ever find the right place?"

"You gave me good directions." He wasn't going to let himself feel flattered. "By the way, that's a great cave. But I'm afraid the tortoise was offended by me, for trespassing."

"Oh, he complains a lot. It comes from being the oldest denizen — he has seen so many seasons, he thinks he knows it all. But he doesn't have the gift of tongues. I wonder how you understood him."

"Well, maybe I just guessed at what he was thinking." Julian couldn't explain it. "I got the idea he was worried about this Monster, too. Incidentally, I think I met it out there. It was digging up the home of one of your neighbors. I kind of believe its bark is worse than its bite, though maybe not to a ground squirrel."

"You must mean the dog." She twitched her tail to brush away that idea. "He's no threat. He's had such an easy life, he's lost most of his instincts. The silly idiot keeps digging one end of a burrow long after you've run out the other. Now, foxes are smarter. Two of them will gang together, one to dig up the front door and the other to watch the back. You have to step lively around foxes."

"You mean you're not afraid of the dog?" Julian felt slightly foolish.

"Of course I am," she told him. "He wants to eat us. But that's only natural — like foxes and coyotes, he was born to hunt. We scuttlers and scurriers were born to out-run, out-leap, out-guess the hunters and may the best of us survive. The Monster is different. He doesn't play the life-game. He never eats what he kills, he just stamps out the burrows and squashes whoever is inside, then goes off snickering and snorting. He destroys for no purpose — that's why he's a Monster and must be stopped. Those men are big enough to do it, if they band together. You'd think they would have big minds, too, but I guess it doesn't work that way."

Julian didn't want to comment on his bosses or their brains. "I guess I'd better get back to my chores," he said, slightly nervous. "You need some fresh water."

"Don't bother," Leaper said. "I never touch the stuff."

"Hold on. Everybody has to drink."

"Not my family. We get the moisture we need from the leaves of the life-tree."

"Oh no," he groaned.

"Never mind, it doesn't matter. My life will soon be over. I'd rather die than live forever in a cage."

"But maybe it won't be forever. Last

month my dad was arguing with Harrison and Whitman. He doesn't like cages, either. He only photographs animals out in the wilds, in their native land. So he told Whitman, 'Why don't you at least put the animals back where you found them after you finish your tests?' And Harrison said, 'We will, we will, in due time.' "

"It will be too late for most of us," Leaper told him. "We were not born to live in captivity."

"Don't give up," Julian begged. "We'll figure something out. Meanwhile, you'd better tell me how I find this life-tree."

"Well, if you insist."

Leaper thought about the smooth, sheer face of the rock and the heat that radiated from it. The coolness of her burrow beneath, the nice chambers she had dug — one for seeds and leaves, others for the children she had hoped to raise. She thought rather proudly of the two extra back doors. (She was somewhat smarter than foxes.)

One of the exit tunnels led to the far side of the rock. It was a shortcut to the life-tree, but it wouldn't be much help to this boy. At last she told him:

"As you know, the cave is surrounded by rocky walls. I go under, but you must go over them.

"Beyond, you'll find a narrow ravine where you will walk on a red carpet. Be careful through there — watch for the snake-that-skips.

"When you come to a place with a roof you can't see, you will find a tree with branches that grow both upward and down-ward. That's the life-tree."

As Julian was about to put her back in her cage, she took her tiny front feet out of her fur and clung to his thumb. "One thing more: Sometimes the Monsters come rav-aging and savaging in packs. If you hear their wild gnashing, you must run!"

9

By ten o'clock that morning Julian had finished his chores. Since it was Sunday, he was free for the rest of the day. When he came out of the lab, he found the sky was being polished by a brisk wind. The Popsicle was standing ready beside the back porch, its red enamel sparkling. He called the motor-bike the "Popsicle" because it was a sweet little machine. Just climbing onto it, he felt the big clinker of doubt inside him begin to split and crumble. A fine day — what better to do than go looking for some crazy leaves?

The breeze was kicking up sand in gusts. He pulled the visor of his helmet down to protect his eyes, but once in a while a flurry would find its way underneath and he would taste sand on his lips. *Eating the desert*, he thought, and laughed out loud, filled with elation to be going his own way, alone.

When he reached the arroyo, he hid the machine deep in the same narrow gully and headed for the cave. It occurred to him that he wouldn't get blisters if he didn't wear boots, so he took them off. Tying them together by their laces, he slung them across his shoulder. With the sand squinching up warm between his toes, he made good time. He wasn't even thinking of monsters when suddenly he heard noises up ahead.

Then he recognized what it was — the blast of music from a boom box. A hundred yards on, he found a picnic in progress, boys and girls from the high school sprawled around a small fire, roasting hot dogs. He knew them all — in a small town, everyone knows everybody.

They yelled greetings at him. "Hey, if it isn't J. X. Jugears."

Julian gave them a careless flip of his hand. He was used to their teasing; they weren't being mean.

"Sit down, have a dog," one of the boys said, trying to be friendly.

"Yeah, you might learn a few things," another one said, and put his arm around a pretty blond girl sitting next to him.

"Get lost," she giggled, "I'm going to be Julian's date. He's going to sit right here. . . ." She patted the ground beside her.

Julian knew she was using him to tease the boy. He never could think of the right thing to say around high school kids, so he just grinned a stupid grin and kept walking.

"What's the matter, aren't we good enough for King Xerxes?"

And a dark-haired girl spoke up — her sister was in Julian's class at middle school. "Don't you know? That 'X' in his name stands for ex-clusive. He prefers his own company."

"How ex-asperating."

"Maybe he's ex-hausted."

"Or ex-pired."

Julian stuttered. "I'm — I'm — on duty. For the lab. I have to — to collect specimens."

"Ex-cuses, ex-cuses," they chanted.

One of the boys said, "Hey, you need a lizard? I'll nail one for you." And he threw his empty pop can at a horned toad clinging to the rock nearby. It ducked over the top and was gone before the can hit.

"I see another!" Then they were all throwing things, yelling. The racket they made, with the radio roaring heavy metal in the background — Julian suddenly realized: These must be the Monsters. Trampling around in packs, no wonder they scare the wildlife. As he went on up the draw, an empty pop can whizzed past his head. One of the girls giggled. "Oooops, sorry about that."

He didn't look back. As soon as he was out of sight beyond the curve of the arroyo, he broke into a fast trot, stubbing his toes on the rocks, ducking down the short dead-end cranny where the life-bush guarded the entrance to the turquoise cave. A quick sweep of the flashlight showed that the tortoise was gone. It was Julian's private hole for the moment.

Like the ugly little toad, he flung himself into the darkness. For a while he lay on his back on the floor, catching his breath, listening to his heart pound.

10

The kids didn't know it, but they had bounced their wisecracks off a very tender spot. Secretly, Julian had always been fond of that "X." He liked to think it stood for *Extra* — that some day he would be an expert at something. For years he had waited for a special talent to appear, even a minor one. Surely, he thought, everybody is born with some sort of gift.

Like Leaper. Inch-for-inch, she was the finest jumper in the desert. Maybe in the entire state of California. Or the whole world. (Did they have kangaroo rats in China? He didn't know.) That's the whole trouble, he thought. *I'm not ex-perienced with rats, except one. And I'd better quit moping in this cave and look for that life-tree.*

But about then he heard the gang of pic-nickers coming up the draw. Let them get past, he thought, and he lay still on the cool rock floor of the cavern. By now he was sure that they were Leaper's monsters, making all that noise, throwing their trash at the denizens. . . . A pop can clattered off a stone not far away and loud voices laughed sky-high. The next second a lizard came hurtling around the life-bush and into the cave. It dived down the nearest hole, which happened to be Julian's collar, burrowing deep in his shirt.

The minute its small cold feet touched his skin, a current of contact flowed be-tween him and the creature. He could sense its chilly reptilian mind, blank with shock,

and quickly sent it a message: "I won't hurt you. I'm a friend of Leaper's."

There was no response, but after a few seconds the scaly feet began to tiptoe back up his chest toward his collar.

"Don't go yet," Julian whispered. "They're still right outside. You don't want them to find this place. Please don't be scared."

Finally he felt a very fine thread of thought from the lizard. "I knoweth not

fear. I cometh from a long line of dino-
saurs."

"Oh, good. I'm glad," he said. "Those
monsters really don't mean any harm.
They're just fooling around. They don't realize they might hurt somebody."

"You referreth to the young human
beings, I suppose? They are a silly lot, clum-
sier than the cave dwellers from whom they
hath descended. Do not confuse these with
the Monster." Coming from the small reptile the word seemed more like "ogre." In
fact, the lizard wasn't speaking English at
all. Julian realized he was listening in lizard, a language ancient and lofty.

"Human beings," his guest went on,
"hath long since lost their agility; it's probably because of the vile water they drinketh
from those metal cylinders. My imbecile
nephew once crawled into one and sipped
the remainder. It made him so dizzy he be-
cameth an easy dinner for the roadrunner."

"Sorry to hear it," Julian told him politely. "Your nephew probably got hold of some beer. I never touch the stuff myself." But he wouldn't have minded some water about then. He had come off in such a hurry he'd forgotten his thermos. "Where do you usually go to get a drink?" he asked.

"Ah, alas. There was a very nice pool that collected in a rock after the last thunderstorm. No more, no more. The ogre hath destroyed it." The lizardy mind shuddered. "Now him I calleth a genuine threat. If I were inclined to be cowardly I would fear him. He is faster than me and bigger than thee."

So Julian was back to starters. He was beginning to feel frustrated by this illusive ogre—monster thing. "What exactly does it look like?"

The lizard, if it wasn't afraid, certainly got nervous thinking about it. The tiny cold feet were doing a small dance on Julian's chest and its mental images came and went like flickers of a strobe light: an impression of armor heavier than a tortoise's shell, of countless terrible toes, of horns and a single round black eye — a big shapeless thing, casting a horrible, shapeless shadow.

"Well, I'll do my best to take care of him if I meet him." Julian tried to sound brisk and fearless. "Right now, I'd better move along. I have to find the life-tree. Leaper needs some leaves from it."

"I'll show thee the way." The lizard peered cautiously out of the open neck of Julian's shirt. "That rock opposite here must be crossed. I don't suppose thou hast suction cups on thy toes?"

"No," Julian admitted, "but I've done some mountain climbing." The walls of the cranny were close enough together that he could brace his back against one and his feet on the other, hitching himself upward step by step. When he crawled out onto the rim of the arroyo, he was instantly swept by the wind. Blowing harder across the long miles of desert, it had picked up more sand — he had to duck his head away from it. The lizard just lowered its tough protective eyelids and tightened the scales around its ear holes.

"Follow me." The lizard skittered down Julian's pantleg and darted away across the rocky earth, rising on its rear legs to run faster. The creature really did resemble a small dinosaur. A quick one. It ducked over

the edge of another gully, and when he caught up, he saw it below. It flicked its tail once, as if to say, *This is it*, and was gone into a hole.

Julian climbed down into the gulch, which was much smaller than the big arroyo. He was glad to get out of the wind, which had made his eyes smart. They even seemed slightly dazzled. Through the windy haze, it looked as if the sand were strewn with rubies!

Scooping up a handful, he saw that the small red chips were actually garnets, not much bigger than the tiny grains on sandpaper you buy at the hardware store. They couldn't be very valuable, and yet, by the hundreds of thousands, they gleamed like a carpet fit for royalty. Maybe, as his mother once said, kings come in all kinds of packages.

The lizard certainly considered itself a member of reptile nobility, dating back sixty million years. Julian had an idea it didn't talk to just anybody. The more he thought about it, the more his spirits lifted. To speak to such a creature, mind-to-mind — you might almost say that took a certain talent. Maybe, Julian thought, he was endowed with something . . . slightly . . . ex-tra, after all.

As Julian walked along, he was starting to get an idea, a kind of dream of the future. It stirred inside him like a small fish in deep water, about to swim to the top when . . .

He saw the rock. He might not have noticed it if the quail hadn't drawn it to his attention. A whole family of them were grouped around it in a circle, muttering as birds do when they are upset. The neat black crests on their heads were drooping with dismay. As he came up, they rushed

off, running in a neat line, parents herding
the young ones into a narrow cleft between
two boulders.

Left alone, Julian puzzled over the rock.
A good-sized slab of stone, it had been hol-
lowed by centuries of weather — storms
and winds and heat and cold — until it was
dish-shaped. This must be the catch-pool
the lizard had mentioned. But it would
never hold water again — it had been broken in two. And finally Julian had to believe
there really was a Monster. Possibly a full-
fledged ogre — a big one. What else could
have cracked such a rock, short of an ele-
phant? A rhinoceros? King Kong?

Keeping a sharper look-out, he moved more slowly up the draw. As always he sensed that he was being watched, but this time the feeling was stronger, more personal. For some reason it made him want to put on his boots. As he finished tying the laces and straightened up, he took a careful look around.

Just as well. Right ahead, coiled under a bush, a snake was staring at him. The same color as the gravel it lay on, it was almost invisible except for the flick of its tongue and the slight quiver of the rattles on its tail. Under strange scaly horns, its eyes were as cold as marbles.

Could the gift of tongues reach across twenty feet of empty space? Julian said aloud, "Hi, there." Then, because possibly the snake had important ancestors, too, he tried a more respectful salutation. "Greetings, O Guardian of the Gulch." That sounded pretty good to him. It didn't impress the snake a bit.

"Listen," he tried again, "I didn't come here to start trouble."

The snake licked its lips, the forked tongue darting, darting.

"All I want," Julian said, "is to come face-to-face with the monstrous ogre who is, I believe, just up the wash."

In one sinuous movement, the snake uncoiled and threw itself sideways, looping off across the ground rapidly, arching its body up and over a few inches with each wriggle until it went down its hole. It left a track on the sand that reminded Julian of Leaper's words: the snake-that-skips.

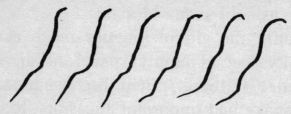

A sidewinder — the most fearsome killer of the desert — and it, too, was scared of the Monster. All at once Julian felt more nervous than ever, maybe because the sun had disappeared behind a whole stack of looming dark clouds and the wind had turned wilder than ever up above the gulch, making a roof — "a roof you can't see" — beneath which the little ravine was quieter. He hoped that meant he'd find the life-tree soon.

Around the next twist in the gully, there it was. Hidden deep between the protecting banks of rock stood an ironwood tree so old that the lower branches had died and slanted downward. Within their shelter some denizen had built a great messy nest of twigs and other things. Julian saw an old shoelace, the tatters of a red kerchief, a brass buckle off a knapsack.

"Anybody home?" he called, not wanting to intrude unannounced. He thought he heard a soft scuttling. Or maybe it was just the wind that raked the upper branches, which grew toward the sky in proper tree

fashion. Tiny leaves were floating down everywhere. Scrambling around, Julian picked enough in a few minutes to fill the empty mustard jar he had brought for the purpose. But when he looked for the lid, it was gone.

"I left it right on that rock," he said out loud. Suspecting what had happened, he called out to the owner of the junky nest, "You bring that back! I need it!"

No answer. Only the sound of the wind.

12

Julian was sore at himself. A naturalist would have known better than to leave things lying loose when there was a pack rat in the neighborhood. The darned little thief was probably using that lid for a coffee table by now. Stuffing a Kleenex in the top of the jar, he put it in his pocket and headed back down the draw, keeping a sharp eye out in all directions. A naturalist wouldn't have almost stepped on that sidewinder.

He wondered if a naturalist would recognize the description of the Monster. Or know where this Black River was? In his mind's eye, Julian could picture the thing rising out of its secret waters, its crusty flanks dripping weeds like some old horror movie. The gruesome black eye would swivel around until it located its prey. Then it would charge, roaring and tearing up the earth with its long claws.

Since he had never run across anything like that in his schoolbooks, he supposed it must be a new species. And that's why Leaper risked her life to bring word of it to the only people who could combat the thing. With what? Machine guns and bazookas? Warfare, stripping the desert of its quiet, with the smell of gunsmoke floating down the arroyo — the thought made Julian shudder. He could almost feel the violence hovering over this peaceful spot.

Or maybe that was just electricity from the oncoming storm. As he hauled the Popsicle out of hiding, the wind was beginning to hurl its own ammunition. Small hard drops of rain slashed his neck and ears, even as he raced away from it. Far off over the rocky rim of the horizon, wild lightning flickered from the big guns of the storm that was moving in.

By the time he got to the lab, Julian was wet as a wet sponge. He slipped in quietly; he didn't want to disturb the night watchman, who might have had orders to keep him out. But the old man was reading a newspaper, eating a sandwich. Julian's own stomach was growling with hunger. And worse than that, his mind rumbled with uneasiness. The minute he opened the door to the lab he sensed that the animals were all dithery. In their cages, the chipmunks chattered nervously and the gopher ran in circles, while the blackbird kept going, "Ick, ick, ick, ick."

Julian hurried to Leaper's cage, but she was slow coming into his hand. "What's the matter?" he said in dismay. "Don't you trust me?"

"It's hard to trust people," she admitted. "Those men have been after me all day, trying to make me talk. Not what I want to say — they keep telling me to speak *their* words. Say 'hello' and say 'I'm a rat' and say 'I can talk.' "

"Maybe you should have played along, just to get them off your case."

"No," she said, "I'd feel foolish. The denizens didn't send me here to show off. Not that I'll ever see them again," she added sadly. "These men will never let me go. The white one said, 'We must try harder!' and the hairy one kept crying, 'We must be doing something wrong. What are we doing wrong?'

"He got so upset he spilled a cup of that hot stuff in his lap. It must have given him a whole lot of those jitters, because he jumped up fast and knocked the chair over. It startled us out of our wits — we're not used to all this fuss. I should never have come here, but at least that's my own doing.

These other creatures never wanted to be here at all. Can't you help us escape?"

"The trouble with that," he tried to explain, "is it's against the law to steal."

"Steal? Us? We don't belong to anyone but ourselves. I walked into that trap of my own free will. I should have the right to walk out again," she told him fiercely. "All you need to do is open the doors of the cages. We'd take our chances on getting home." The thought made her heart beat faster.

Julian could sense it. He could feel her wanting and wishing and depending on him. The dilemma nearly tore him in two: If he got arrested for rat-lifting, it would be a Black Mark against him forever, maybe even keep him from getting a scholarship to college some day and learning to be excellent. And yet, it was true what she said — even a wild creature has its rights. These animals hadn't hurt anyone or broken any laws. So who was to say they shouldn't be let go? Only Whitman and Harrison — they had made themselves judge and jury. They were the only ones he had to worry about. If only he weren't too young to outwit them. . . .

Julian almost got mad at himself. "It's time I stopped being 'too young,'" he thought, "and started being 'old enough.' At least old enough to use my noggin." His dad had great faith in J. X.'s noggin.

So think! Glancing around, he saw the video camera still set up. He knew how to run it — his father had taught him.

"Maybe," he said out loud, "just maybe . . ."

13

By now the rain was coming down as if the sky had tipped and spilled. When he got back to the lab Julian was wetter than two sponges. But the package was dry in a piece of plastic he had wrapped around it. Carefully he took out the videotape — it was one from his father's supply. He removed the tape in the camera, which belonged to the Research Center, of course, and replaced it with his own.

Then he turned on the lights, all the while

hoping fiercely that the two researchers would be busy watching television in their apartments and not looking out the windows. When he got the camera focused, he let Leaper out of her cage and said, "Now, if you can, just explain it — the reason you feel you should be let go."

Her nose twitched as if to imply that she'd be glad to. Hopping over to the one-eared creature, she squeaked, but nothing happened. It didn't seem to be listening.

"Wait a minute while I turn on the machine. Let's see, I've watched them do it often enough — " He was pushing buttons.

Leaper didn't understand. "Machine" was an odd word to her, but she realized that it meant the thing wasn't alive after all. Yet it seemed to chirp a greeting, and its face flowed with green lines as if anxious to begin. When she spoke, words popped up on the screen:

> "I am Leaper, proud member of a family of Leapers and representative of the denizens of the desert. I entered a trap on purpose, so that I could talk to the human beings here. They are the only ones big enough to fight the Miserable Morbid Monster of the Black River."

Julian wanted to advise her not to exaggerate too much, but she was chattering on so fast he couldn't get a word in edgewise.

78

"I now see that the men who brought me here are not interested in helping us. Therefore, I am going to leave. No one stole me, for I belong to no one. If I choose to go, it's my right. The other captives in these cages never gave their permission to be here at all. They were kept against their will — the chipmunk, the blackbird, the mouse. So now we are returning to our homes."

Julian got it all on tape. By now he was growing a bit uneasy about what he'd got himself into. But it was too late for second thoughts. Turning off the video camera, he punched a button and the computer made a written copy of Leaper's statement. This printout he left on Harrison's desk. But the tape, which showed her actually talking — that he wrapped in the plastic bag again and put inside his shirt. People would be skeptical; they'd say it was some sort of trick. But he thought his father would believe him. Anyway, it was the only protection he would have when his bosses found the specimens were gone. By now he was busy opening cages.

The blackbird flew off out the window into the rainy night.

The chipmunk dashed off across the street to the trees in the park.

The Gila monster glowered at him so meanly, he left that alone, but the rest of them — the spiders and garter snakes and the moody bat — he turned loose into the wet darkness. They could take care of themselves.

"But you," he told Leaper, "are going to need a lift. It's a long, long way back to your home."

She wasn't listening. Poised on the table, her head was cocked toward the door. Then he heard them, too — voices outside.

". . . must be that boy again!"

". . . had enough of this. I'm going to fire him. He has disobeyed orders once too often."

They had the outer door open and were coming along the hall. Julian stood frozen on the spot. But Leaper was a quick thinker. With one kick of those marvelous hind feet, she flung herself up onto his shoulder. Clinging to his ear with her front paws, she hurled at his mind a single word:

"Run!"

And he did — out the back door, into the night. Behind them they heard the men crying out.

"Look at those cages — they're all empty!"

But Leaper was tweaking his ear. *"Jump. Sideways!"*

Julian ducked away from the lighted door.

"Hide!"

He plunged into the black shadows behind a Dumpster, hardly breathing as the two men bolted out the door. They flicked on the parking-lot lights, flooding the whole area with a blue-white glow.

"He's probably taken the specimens home for pets." Harrison stood there with the rain dripping off his beard. "I knew he was too young to be allowed into a laboratory."

"Well, come along," Whitman snapped. "It isn't far to his house."

As their footsteps slushed off into the distance, Julian took a deep breath. They wouldn't find anyone home. His father was still away on the field trip and his mother, who was a nurse, was sitting up with a sick old lady on the other side of town. He had left her a note so she wouldn't worry: "Spending the night with a friend."

The word warmed him all over. To have a real friend, even one who was two inches high, well, it was the first time it had ever happened to him. Cautiously, he stood up. "I think it's safe now."

"*Oh no, oh no, oh no!*" Leaper's whole small body was pouring out a message of terror. "*Not safe! Not safe!*"

"But I don't see anybody."

"Over there!" she screamed. "It's the Monster!"

"It's the horned creature with the terrible feet that go in circles!" Leaper was hanging onto the boy's ear so hard her claws dug in like needles. "Don't go any closer!"

But he wouldn't be warned, this young human being she had come to like, who had brought her food and opened the door of her cage. He was making a sound like "ha-ha-ha." She felt confused and belittled, as if she'd been called *stupid*.

"It's only a motor-bike. A machine," he told her. "It's not alive. And this is just a helmet to protect my head." He held up the round goggle-eye and Leaper saw that it was only an empty shell like those of long-gone tortoises that lay around the desert.

"A big motorcycle is pretty heavy," he went on. "I can see how it could do a lot of damage. But not on purpose — it isn't evil. It isn't anything, just a vehicle to ride on. And right now it can get you home in a hurry, if you're willing."

Leaper's heart was fluttering so hard she couldn't think. She only knew that she would surely die if she stayed in this strange place. Everything was so bright, even though it was night — she felt dread-fully exposed. And the ground was covered with a dark rigid crust, so hard that it glistened in the rain. You could never burrow into that. The trees were too tall. They smelled strange. No matter what it took, she wanted to go home to her own world.

"Would it help for you to duck into my

pocket?" Julian offered, as he eased onto the awful creature.

"No." She wanted to stay free to jump off at the first sign of trouble.

"Don't do that," he warned. "We'll be traveling near the highway — that's your 'Black River' — and it carries a lot of traffic. On a night like this, the drivers would never see you. You could get run over. But if you stick with me, I promise I'll get you home safe."

Her keen ears picked up the sounds of heavy steps squelching back toward them through the night. She had no choice, although it took all her courage to say "All right."

He kicked the fearsome machine and it began its awful roar. Leaper almost panicked. She clung to her perch on his shoulder, wondering how the boy could stand it. But he liked it. He was filled with warmth. As they raced off into the night, she sensed that he was lifted by a kind of joy such as

she felt when she had escaped an owl.

Or was that another silly mistake? Maybe his inner throbbing didn't come from a heart at all, but some kind of machinery that got plugged in when he sat on the Monster. He seemed to become part of the thing, his hands stuck to its horns, his legs clamped around its flanks. She tried to reach his mind, to feel what he was thinking, but it came to her all scrambled.

15

Julian was, in fact, riding a wind of excitement. Even though he was in deep trouble, his heart kept telling him he was right. Never mind the two men back there waiting to skin him alive, he felt one hundred percent happy about those empty cages.

And he was relieved to know the identity of the Monster at last. He could have kicked himself for missing the clues. The many toes were the tread of the tires, and the horns were handlebars. Of course. *I was even starting to be slightly afraid of it my-self,* he thought, laughing some more. But he had to be careful not to insult Leaper. He knew his thoughts might carry to her small quick brain, so he hid them and concentrated on threading his way through the darkness, avoiding the bushes that rose in the cone of his headlight. He just hoped fervently that he wouldn't run over any denizens.

Sorry, he was sorry for every bit of damage ever done by some thoughtless character on a motor-bike. He would reassure her that he, at least, had never crushed anyone's home. But she must know that by now. After all, he had saved her life — his spirit yelled great cheers over that.

When he reached the arroyo, he didn't bother stowing the bike in the ravine; he just laid it down among the dry bushes behind the big blank signboard. "We still have a way to go," he advised. "Don't leave me."

And he was slightly worried when Leaper didn't answer.

The sand was wet and firm to walk on, but he couldn't see two inches ahead. He kept blundering into rocks — good thing he had brought his Big Beam again. He switched it on, explaining to her, "People can't see in the dark. We aren't familiar with your world. We don't know much about life-bushes, so we might step on them by mistake. All rocks look alike to us. We'd never dream that one was a bird's drinking dish. But we don't mean any harm. . . ." The flashlight had picked up two small bright eyes out there shining in the rain.

"*Oh don't, don't, don't!*" Leaper implored. "That's my sister. Can't you see, you're blinding her. She can't move. The owl will snatch her, the owl, the owl!"

Julian flicked the light off fast. He privately doubted that an owl would be out on a night like this, but —

Leaper heard his thought. "Oh, yes, he will. All creatures have to eat whether it's raining or not. We live by nature's rules. But you break the rules."

Her mind was streaming sadness now. "Maybe you don't mean to, maybe you can't help it. Because I know now, you're a machine. Like the thing with the green face — that was a listening machine. And those men, they were capturing machines. The Monster is a trampling machine. No wonder nobody would listen to me — I've been talking to creatures that aren't even alive." And with that, she took a sudden leap off into the darkness — three feet, nine-and-a-half inches. Out and down and gone.

Julian was left standing there, stunned. He couldn't even turn on the flashlight to look for her; he didn't want to put the whole neighborhood at risk. Into the lashing, slashing night he called, "Come back! Leaper, please come back!" Then, in an absolute fury, he yelled, "I AM TOO ALIVE!"

Drenched, cold, too tired to think, he started to turn back. But the lightning was all around now, and the open face of the desert is not safe to travel in such a storm. One flash showed him a familiar chimney of rock, and he stumbled toward it. Down on hands and knees, he crawled into the turquoise cave. He couldn't think of it as his, not anymore. But he was going to borrow it one last time. Curling in a ball, he lay there, aching.

"If I were a machine," he told nobody in particular, "I would turn myself off."

16

Stupid. That was the worst of it, he felt dumb. A nobody. Julian Ex-pelled Jones, never going to graduate from school or go on to bigger things. And it served him right, trying to be a hero with his flashlight and his bike and his ignorance. It was luck that he hadn't ridden all over a lot of denizens. "Me," he said aloud in the darkness. "I am their Monster!"

Curled up tight, in a cold knot, he began to comprehend. In his mind, he shrank down and down until he was only two inches tall. He imagined the desert, first quiet and safe, and then in the distance he pictured a cloud of dust, growing bigger. And bigger. And from the dust came the loud roar of a band of huge dark figures, bouncing and bumping across the land, crushing the bushes and wiping out the small burrows and everyone in them, bashing the rocks, running down a denizen here and there as it tried to flee in terror. His mind's eye multiplied the bikers by the dozens, as they would be on the day of the big cross-country race. They'd come screeching their gears, pouring smoke from their exhausts as they raged across this peaceful land — and for what reason? Nothing that Leaper would understand. She wouldn't know what "winning" meant. And what, after all, was a prize worth, if it meant the loss of your friends?

He'd lost her, for sure. The only friend he had. No one but Leaper had ever made him feel important. She had given him dreams, the kind that beckon you toward the future. The word "naturalist" was stuck in his head like a seed; it had almost taken root. He had pictured himself talking to creatures all over the world, discussing their problems, fighting their monsters. As if it were a thing he was born to do.

And he'd flunked out. He'd failed the life-test, the imagination-exam. When he finally slipped into a wretched restless doze, he dreamed he was in a kindergarten class and Leaper was the teacher. She was trying to get him to spell the word "friend." But he kept getting it wrong.

"F-r-e-n-d?"

"No, no, that's not right. Wake up, wake up!" she cried.

In a groggy haze he opened his eyes to find it wasn't entirely a dream. Two tiny stickly feet had hold of his ear.

"*Wake up!*" Her mind had sharp edges of worry. "You must get out of here. The water is coming."

"So what else is new?" Julian grumbled.

"The big, big water," she insisted. "It will fill this cave. You must get out quickly or you'll drown."

He sat up sorely. "Machines don't die. They're not alive, remember?"

Leaper hopped up and down on his shoulder. "I decided I was wrong about that. Will you come on?"

"What gave you a clue?"

"It was your ear." She pinched it again and he winced. "See, it has feeling," she said. "It even bleeds when my claws dig in. It turns pink whenever the men scold you. It's a good ear; if it were slightly larger it would be perfect. Now, will you hurry?"

Julian felt himself begin to smile. She had come here just to rescue him. It began to turn into a full-scale grin of the heart. As he crawled forth into the racket of the storm, he asked, "Can I give you a ride to the top of the rock?"

"No, no. My home will be safe. But I

couldn't stand by and let you be trapped." There was a last flutter of a word, ". . . friend . . ." It was almost lost in the night as she leaped away.

He had to make sure she'd be okay. Briefly he turned on the flash. When he located her hole at the base of the rock, she was already inside, rapidly shoving and packing the dirt from within to fill the opening. In a few seconds, you couldn't have guessed there was ever a burrow there.

And now Julian could hear a roaring noise above the rain. It made the hairs rise on the back of his neck — the ugly sound of a flash flood pouring down the arroyo. As fast as he could, he went up the rockface as he had done before, bracing his feet on the opposite wall.

He could picture what was happening: rainwater from the far-off points of the horizon was rushing down the little gullies into the larger ravines, then into the big arroyo where it had turned into a whole, sudden river. He'd barely scrambled out on top of the bank when the flood struck, crashing against the walls of the gulch, filling it almost to the rim. Pouring on past in the darkness, it sounded like a terrible torrent.

Julian sat shivering at the thought of what might have happened if he'd been caught in the cave. Moping and feeling sorry for himself, he could have lost his whole future — right down the wash. Now, as he hunched there, wet and cold, he began to feel wonderful, as if the flood were carrying off all the misery and mistakes and worry. There wasn't enough time to waste being gloomy.

He had a life to live!

17

When the storm finally subsided, the pale light of early dawn showed the clouds churning off southward, leaving the air fresh and cool as lemonade. Julian looked around in wonder — it was as if he had come into a whole new place. The flood had left the arroyo clean. All the tin cans were gone, the charred embers of dead campfires. Old tracks were swept away, leaving the sand smooth as a blank page on which to write new histories.

Rocks had been carried down from far

above, tossed and dashed and rearranged like new furniture. Some of them had natural saucer shapes that had caught the last of the rainwater. And as Julian watched, slowly the denizens came forth to drink.

Small birds flew in, clustering and gulping and dashing away as larger birds arrived. The quail and her brood surrounded one rocky dish. A mouse shared another with a lizard who looked familiar. A large jackrabbit hopped by, then lifted his head sharply, the long pink ears swiveling to catch some sound that sent him bounding

away. A few seconds later, through the early morning twilight, a fox came slipping along. That sent all the denizens scattering in a hurry.

A tough world, Julian thought, as he watched. Always a struggle to see who's the quickest, the fittest, the smartest. *And that's what I must learn, to do my best.* He felt ready.

As he stood up and stretched, the first rays of the sun reached out to warm away his shivers. Climbing down, he looked for Leaper's hole, just to talk one more time. But there was no sign of it. She was sleeping in, after a long, hard night. The cave was almost buried, too. The flood had rolled a large boulder across the mouth, leaving a hole barely large enough for the tortoise to crawl in. For a minute, Julian was sorry. But then, he wasn't. It would keep the place safe forever from the rock hunters, so there would always be a haven for the denizens.

As for himself, it was time to stop hiding

out. If Leaper could dare to ride her Monster, he could face Harrison and Whitman. He'd have to speak up firmly, as one should who has the gift of tongues. To make them listen to him, he would offer them something they wanted — the tape he had made of Leaper. He'd make them see that he had good reasons for what he'd done — that he was a good listener, better than certain researchers who heard without understanding. He was old enough to plan a future. For one way or another, Julian was determined to go all the way to college and get his degree of Ph.X.N. (for Ex-tremely Ex-cellent Naturalist).

Back at the highway he found the Popsicle, splattered and muddy, but safe above the waters. He was glad to see it. None of this was the bike's fault; it was all a matter of how it was ridden. Yesterday's monster could turn into today's rescuer — ask Leaper. No, it was all up to him personally, J. X. Jones, to be horrid or to be a hero. A decision of the brain, and he thought he'd better start using his.

Stopping beside the soggy sign, he could now make out the faded words: WATCH FOR FLASH FLOODS. With his marking pen, he started to trace them more strongly — it was a good warning. And then he thought of a better message.

Whistling softly between his teeth, he formed the letters neatly:

Not bad, not bad. He hoped nobody would think he had misspelled *that*. As he turned and headed for home, he noticed that the life-bushes were already starting to green up.

ABOUT THE AUTHOR

Annabel Johnson has written more than 20 books for young adults, including *The Grizzly*, which won the William Allen White Children's Book Award.

Mrs. Johnson has spent many winters camping in the Mojave desert with her husband. Her love for that part of the country as well as her acquaintance with many "denizens of the desert" inspired this story. *I Am Leaper* is her first book for Scholastic.